www.BillieBBrownBooks.com

Billie B. Brown Books

First American Edition 2021
Kane Miller, A Division of EDC Publishing
Original Title: Billie B Brown: *The Honey Bees*
Text copyright © 2020 Sally Rippin
Illustration copyright © 2020 Aki Fukuoka
Series design copyright 2020 Hardie Grant Egmont
First published in Australia by Hardie Grant Egmont

For information contact:
Kane Miller, A Division of EDC Publishing
P.O. Box 470663
Tulsa, OK 74147-0663
www.kanemiller.com
www.usbornebooksandmore.com

Library of Congress Control Number: 2020937605

Printed and bound in the United States of America
1 2 3 4 5 6 7 8 9 10

ISBN: 978-1-68464-219-9

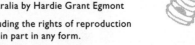

Billie B. Brown

The Honey Bees

By Sally Rippin

Illustrated by Aki Fukuoka

Kane Miller

A DIVISION OF EDC PUBLISHING

Chapter One

Billie B. Brown has two big eyes, two shaky knees and one best friend by her side. Do you know what the "B" in Billie B. Brown stands for?

Bees!

Buzzing, zooming, stinging bees!

Billie and Jack hide under the table. Other kids are hiding too. Do you know what they are hiding from? That's right. Three buzzing bees are flying around the classroom.

Sam jumps up onto
a desk. "I'll kill them!"
he shouts. He picks
up a book and tries
to hit a bee.

"**No, stop!**" comes a
loud voice.

Billie peeks out
from under the desk.
In the doorway stands
the new girl, Sara.

Sara has only been in
Billie's class for two days.
She has moved here
from the country.

"Don't hurt them!"
Sara shouts again.

Billie frowns and looks up at Sara. "But they will sting us!" Billie says.

"No, they won't," Sara says. "Not if you leave them alone." She walks over to the classroom window. She opens it wide. Soon the bees fly outside. Right past Sara's nose!

Billie crawls
out from
under
the desk.
"Wow, you are brave,"
she says to Sara.

Sam climbs down from
the desk. He is annoyed he
didn't get to be the hero
today. Everyone stands
around the new girl.

"Bees aren't scary," Sara says. "We had bees on our farm. Bees are good."

"Sara is right," says Ms. Walton. Everyone looks up as their teacher comes into the classroom. "We need to protect our bees."

"What's so special about bees?" Jack grumbles.

He is the only one left hiding under the desk. He climbs out to stand next to Billie.

Ms. Walton smiles. "Good question," she says. "This week we will talk about ways to look after our planet. Who would like to find out why bees are so important?"

Billie shoots up her hand.
"**Me!**" she says. She smiles
at the new girl. "And can
Sara be my partner?"

Sara smiles
and her cheeks
turn pink.

Jack's cheeks turn pink
too. But he is
not smiling!

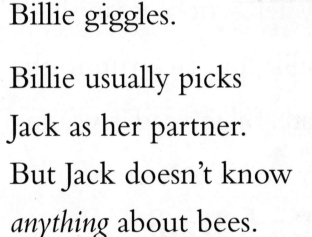

"Oh, and Jack
of course!"
Billie giggles.

Billie usually picks
Jack as her partner.
But Jack doesn't know
anything about bees.

Chapter Two

When school is finished, Billie and Jack run to the gate. Billie's dad is waiting to walk them home.

"Dad, Dad!"

shouts Billie.

"Our class is doing projects on saving the planet. The new girl is in our group. Can she come over?"

Billie looks around the schoolyard for Sara. "There she is," Billie says. "We had bees in our classroom and she wasn't even scared!"

"Sure!" says Billie's dad.

"I'll go ask her mom.

How are you, Jack?"

He messes up Jack's hair.

Jack **shrugs** and smooths

his hair down again.

Billie's dad asks Sara's
mom if Sara can
come over.

"That would be lovely,"
Sara's mom says.
"I'll pick her up just
before dinner."

Sara walks home
with Billie and Jack.
Billie talks the whole way.

Sara talks a lot too.
She tells Billie all
about living on a farm.
It sounds so exciting!

"Wow!" Billie says.
"Sara had her own
horse! How cool is
that, Jack?"

"Pretty cool, I guess,"
Jack says. But he doesn't
look at them.

When they get home,
Jack keeps walking
towards his house.
Jack lives next door.

"Hey, Jack!" Billie says. "We have to work on our project!"

"I'll do it later," Jack says, sounding grumpy. "I'm a bit **tired** today."

"Is he OK?" Sara asks.

Billie shrugs. "Don't worry," she tells Sara. "He's just **shy** sometimes."

But Billie knows
something is not right.
She and Jack have been
friends for a long time.
And no one knows Jack
as well as Billie!

One part of her wants
to go see if he's OK.
The other part of her
is excited to work on a
project with Sara.

Billie decides she will
find a way to cheer
him up later.

Chapter Three

Billie and Sara sit at the computer. They find out lots of things they can do to look after their planet.

Billie writes down " Я, Я, Я."

Billie's mom walks over with baby Noah on her hip. "What does that stand for?" she says.

"**Reduce, reuse, recycle,**" Billie says. "We have to buy less stuff, Mom!"

"That's true," Billie's mom says.

"We recycle what we can. But we can all do better."

"On our farm, we grew vegetables," Sara says. "And had compost bins for our scraps. We kept honey bees, and chickens for eggs."

"We grow vegetables,"
says Billie. "And we have
chickens, too. Hey, Mom!
We should get honey bees!"

"Oh, I don't know …"
says her mom. But she isn't
really listening anymore.
Noah is getting **restless**.
He wants to play on the
computer too!

"But the bees are dying," says Billie. "Sara and I watched a video about it on the internet. If all the bees die there will be no more food! Bees pollinate the flowers so they can grow into fruit and vegetables. We have to save them, Mom! We need to get a **beehive!**"

"We are as busy as bees here already, Billie," her mom says. She jiggles Noah up and down to stop him crying. Then she leaves to give him his dinner.

"Mom obviously doesn't care about saving the planet," Billie huffs. "I know! The **school** should get a beehive."

"Good idea!" says Sara.
"My dad can help.
He knows how to
look after bees."

"This is the best idea
ever," Billie says. "Let's go
next door and tell Jack."

Billie and Sara run
out to the backyard.
They climb into
Jack's yard.

"Jack! Jack!" Billie yells.

Jack comes to the
back door.

"Sara and I have
the **best** idea for
Ms. Walton," Billie says.

"We should get a beehive
at school!"

Jack frowns. His face
turns very red. "That's
a stupid idea!" he says.
"We don't need bees at
school."

"We need to save the bees, Jack!" Billie says. "Why are you so **scared** of bees anyway? Sara says they won't hurt you."

"Bees are **horrible!**" Jack yells. "And I'm *not* scared of them, OK? I don't want to be in your group anyway!" He runs back into his house.

"What's up with him?"
Sara says.

"I have *no* idea," Billie
says. "But he doesn't have
to be so rude."

"Come on," says Sara. She puts her arm around Billie's shoulder. "My mom will be here soon."

They walk back to Billie's house. Billie feels her tummy **bubble** with anger. *What is going on with Jack?* she thinks.

Can you guess?

Chapter Four

That night, Billie's dad
tucks her into bed.
Billie tells him how rude
Jack was. "I don't know
if I can be friends with
him anymore," she says,
frowning.

"Oh, Billie," her dad says. "Jack is allergic to bees. He was stung once when he was little. He had to spend three days in the hospital. No wonder he's scared of them."

"Oh no! Poor Jack!" Billie says. She sits up suddenly.

"But why didn't he just tell me? I'm his best friend!"

"Well, maybe he didn't feel like your best friend today?" Billie's dad says. "After all, you seemed very busy with the new girl. Maybe Jack isn't just scared of bees. Maybe he's scared you don't want to be his friend anymore?"

"Oh dear," says Billie. "You're right. I haven't been a good friend today. I didn't even notice how scared he was. Maybe he won't want to be *my* friend anymore?"

Billie's dad kisses her forehead. "Don't worry, Billie," he says. "You'll find a way to make things right. You always do."

Billie lies in the
dark and **worries**.
Worries always feel
much bigger in the dark.
But Billie B. Brown is lots
of things. She is brave.
She is brilliant. She is
bold. Billie B. Brown
may not know how
to save the planet yet.
But she does know how
to save a friendship.

The next morning, Billie
quickly gets dressed for
school. She runs out into
the backyard.

You know
where she
is going,
don't you?

"Jack! Jack!" Billie calls.

Jack opens the door.

He is still in his pajamas.
"I'm not going to
school today," he says
in a **grumpy** voice.
"I don't feel well."

"Oh, Jack," Billie says.
She gives him a big hug.
"You should have told
me you were allergic
to bees. I would be
scared of bees too if
I was allergic to them."

Jack looks **surprised**. "Really?" he says. "But you're not scared of anything, Billie!"

Billie smiles. "That's not true," she says.

"Last night I was scared you didn't want to be my friend anymore."

Jack laughs. "That's funny," he says. "I was scared you didn't want to be *my* friend anymore! Because I'm not as brave as Sara."

"That's just silly," Billie grins. "You'll *always* be my best friend.

Now get dressed," she says. "We need you to help us with our project!"

"But don't you want to put a beehive in the school?" Jack says, nervously.

"Nah," shrugs Billie. "I reckon compost is a *much* better idea. And we can use it to plant flowers for the bees. No one is allergic to compost!"

The Bad Butterfly
By Sally Rippin

The Soccer Star
By Sally Rippin

The Midnight Feast
By Sally Rippin

The Second-best Friend
By Sally Rippin

The Extra-special Helper
By Sally Rippin

The Beautiful Haircut
By Sally Rippin

The Big Sister
By Sally Rippin

The Spotty Vacation
By Sally Rippin

The Birthday Mix-up
By Sally Rippin

The Secret Message
By Sally Rippin

The Little Lie
By Sally Rippin

The Best Project
By Sally Rippin

The Deep End
By Sally Rippin

The Copycat Kid
By Sally Rippin

The Night Fright
By Sally Rippin

The Missing Tooth
By Sally Rippin

The Bully Buster
By Sally Rippin

The Grumpy Neighbor
By Sally Rippin

The Hat Parade
By Sally Rippin

The Honey Bees
By Sally Rippin

Collect them all!

Don't forget the book starring both Jack AND Billie!

Billie B. Brown & Hey Jack!
The Book Buddies
By Sally Rippin